LAYLA and the BOTS

MAKING WAVES

written by
Vicky Fang

illustrated by
Christine Nishiyama

BRANCHES

SCHOLASTIC INC.

For my mom. —VF
To Rachel, for taking a chance on me. —CN

Text copyright © 2022 by Vicky Fang
Illustrations copyright © 2022 by Christine Nishiyama

Library of Congress Cataloging-in-Publication Data

Names: Fang, Vicky, author. | Nishiyama, Christine, illustrator. |
Fang, Vicky. Layla and the Bots;
4. Title: Making waves / written by Vicky Fang; illustrated by Christine Nishiyama.
Description: New York: Branches/Scholastic Inc., 2022. | Series: Layla and the Bots; 4 |
Summary: Layla and the Bots visit the Surfside Rescue Center where they meet a dolphin named Splash, who will only eat when the music is playing, but is very picky about the music—so Layla and the Bots build a machine that uses the sound waves Splash communicates with to change the music.

Identifiers: LCCN 2021013093 |
ISBN 9781338583007 (paperback) | ISBN 9781338583014 (library binding)
Subjects: LCSH: Robots—Juvenile fiction. | Sound waves—Juvenile fiction. |
Dolphins—Juvenile fiction. | Animal sounds—Juvenile fiction. | CYAC:
Robots—Fiction. | Sound waves—Fiction. | Dolphins—Fiction. | Animal sounds—Fiction.
Classification: LCC PZ7.1.F3543 Mak 2022 | DDC [Fic]—dc23
LC record available at https://lccn.loc.gov/2021013093

10 9 8 7 6 5 4 3 2 1   22 23 24 25 26

Printed in China 62
First edition, February 2022

Illustrated by Christine Nishiyama
Edited by Rachel Matson
Book design by Maria Mercado

TABLE OF CONTENTS

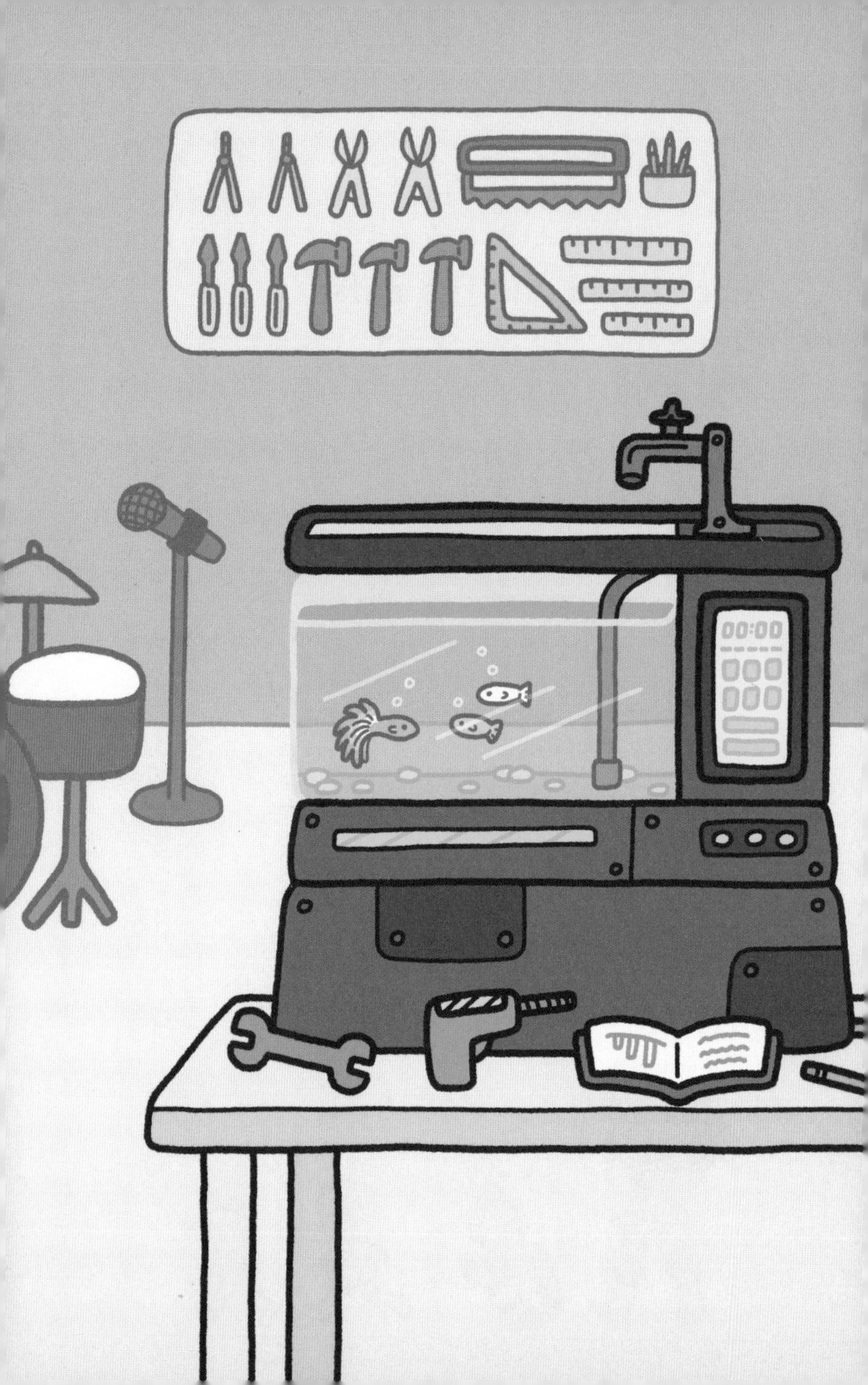
00:00

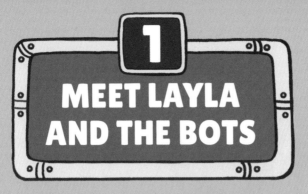

1
MEET LAYLA AND THE BOTS

This is Layla. She is an inventor. And a rock star.

These are the Bots.

BEEP

BOOP

BOP

They are part of Layla's crew.

Beep knows things.

BEEP.
This special wire
lights up!

Boop builds things.

More wire?

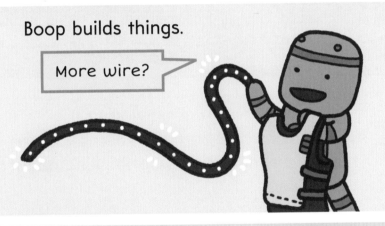

Bop codes things.

Blinky-blinky!

[dive]
→
blink!

Layla and the Bots play music in their town of Blossom Valley.

This week, they are playing at a fundraiser for the Surfside Rescue Center. This is why they can't stop thinking about ocean things . . .

Like sea creatures,

BEEP.
The whale shark
is the biggest fish
in the world.

submarines,

Down we go . . .

and surfing!

Wee-hoo!

Whenever Layla and the Bots get together, awesome things happen.

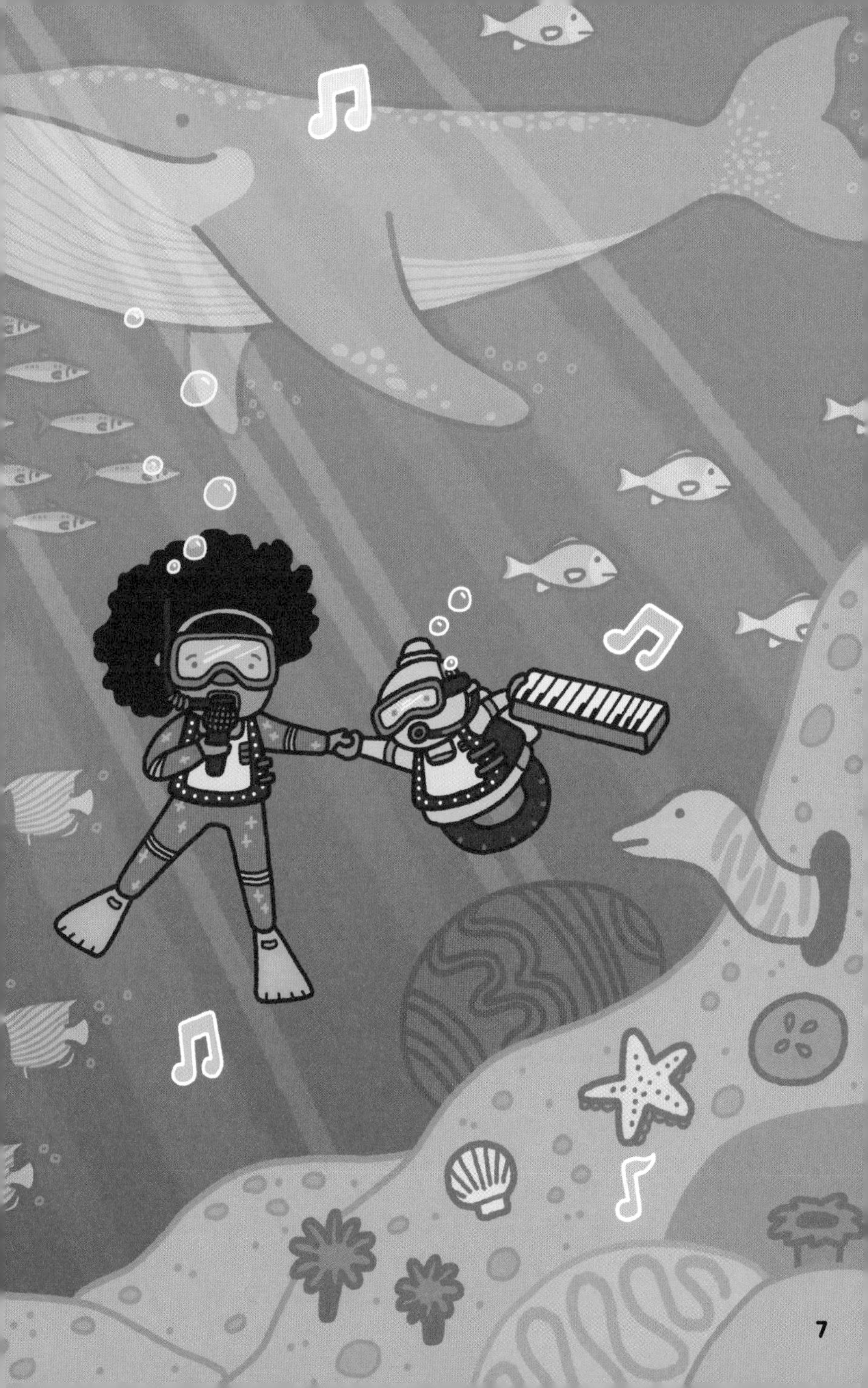

2

SEA SICK

On Thursday morning, Layla and the Bots are at the Surfside Rescue Center. The center's fundraiser is in three days! But right now, they are getting a tour from one of the animal doctors.

Hi! I'm Dr. Sophie. Sunday's fundraiser will raise money to feed and care for hurt animals. We help the animals get better and release them back into the ocean when they are ready.

9

Dr. Sophie introduces them to some of the animals. First, they meet Brutus the sea turtle. He has a hurt flipper.

Dr. Sophie gives Brutus vitamins.

He is healing well.

Yay-yay!

Next, they meet a sea lion named Bella. She was tangled in a fishing net. The animal doctors found her and untangled her.

Bella is doing great. We're releasing her back into the ocean today!

Great news!

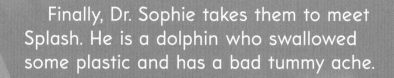

Finally, Dr. Sophie takes them to meet Splash. He is a dolphin who swallowed some plastic and has a bad tummy ache.

Why did a dolphin eat plastic?

BEEP.
Plastic garbage pollutes our oceans. Many marine animals eat the plastic by mistake.

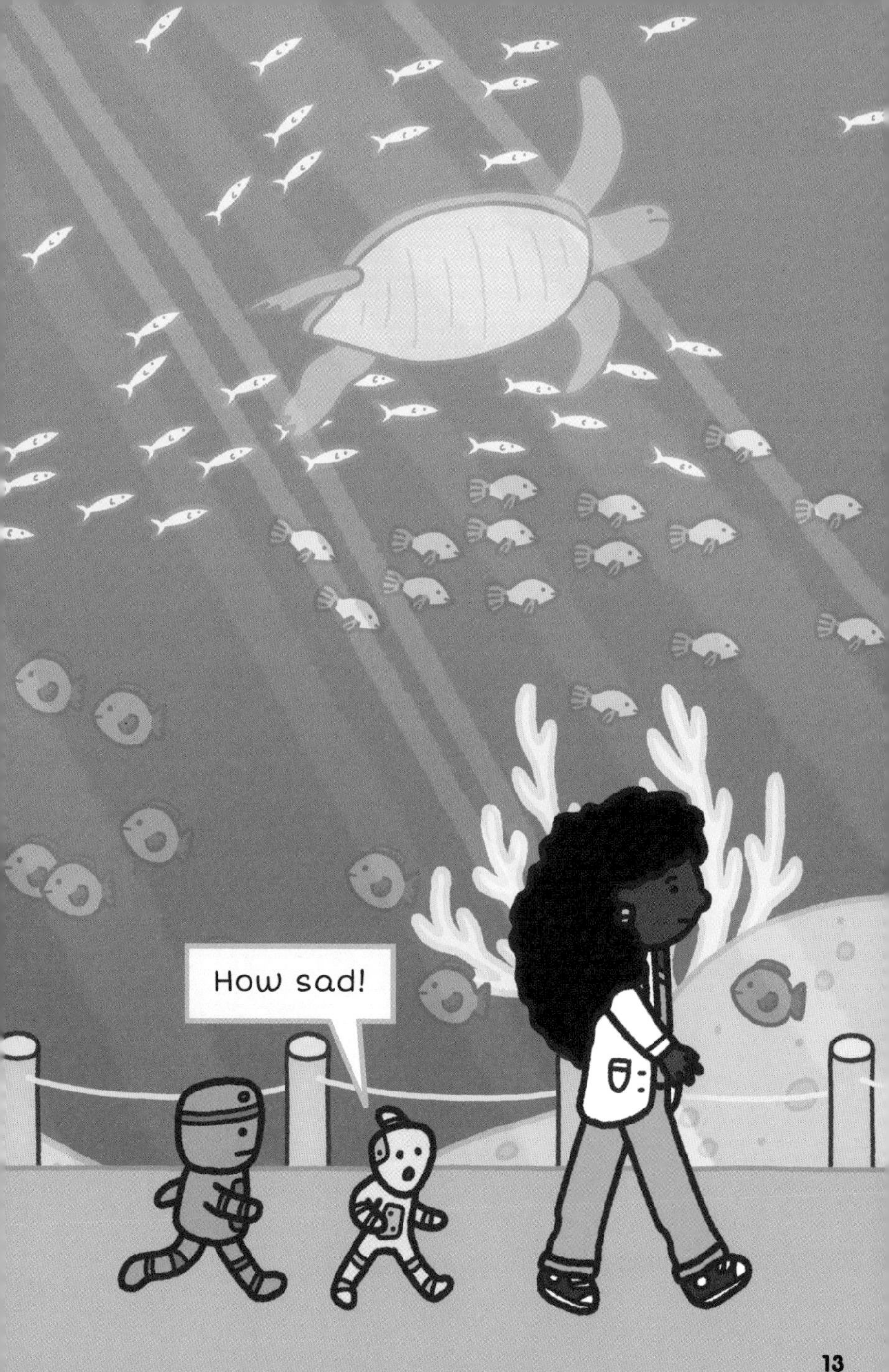
How sad!

When they see Splash, he is swimming
back and forth, squeaking loudly.
Dr. Sophie looks worried.

Why is he squeaking?

Splash squeaks
when he is unhappy.

Is he unhappy because of his tummy ache?

Squeak! Squeak!

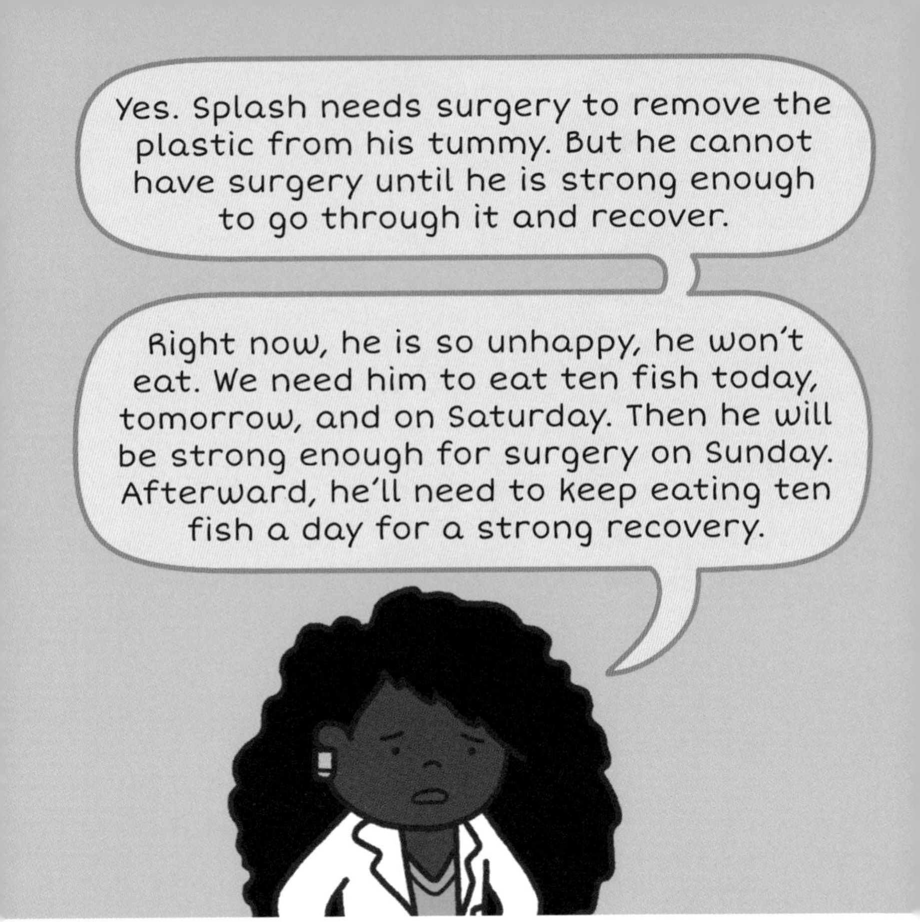
Yes. Splash needs surgery to remove the plastic from his tummy. But he cannot have surgery until he is strong enough to go through it and recover.
Right now, he is so unhappy, he won't eat. We need him to eat ten fish today, tomorrow, and on Saturday. Then he will be strong enough for surgery on Sunday. Afterward, he'll need to keep eating ten fish a day for a strong recovery.

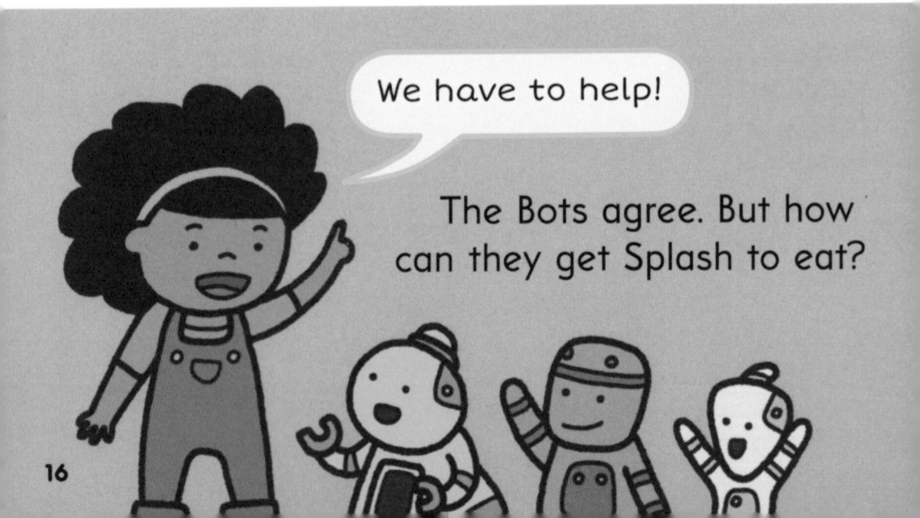
We have to help!
The Bots agree. But how can they get Splash to eat?

3

SOUND BITE

Layla watches Splash swimming back and forth.

We need to learn more about Splash.

But how?

Try feeding him!

17

Beep tries asking.

Boop tries wiggling.

Bop tries singing.

Suddenly, Splash stops squeaking!

Shh, listen!

Bop stops singing. Splash starts squeaking again.

Bop, keep singing!

Squeak! Squeak!

Bop goes over to Splash and starts singing. Immediately, Splash stops squeaking. Then, he starts clicking!

Splash clicks when he is happy!

That's it! Splash likes music!

Click!
Click!
Click!

Splash waves his tail.
Boop throws him a fish,
and he gulps it down.

Wow! Splash will eat
if he hears music!

This gives Layla an idea.

4
CHANNEL SURFING

Layla and Dr. Sophie set up a music player for Splash.

Then Dr. Sophie leaves to check on the other animals.

Boop points the speakers at the pool.
Bop starts the music. Splash starts clicking!

He eats another fish.

But then Splash stops clicking.

What happened?

Squeak!
Squeak!

Layla frowns.

Try different music, Bop!

24

Bop changes the music. He tries jazz, then disco.

Splash likes the disco music!

Click! Click! Click!

He eats two more fish.

Then Splash stops clicking and starts squeaking again.

Squeak! Squeak!

Bop changes the music to pop. Splash likes the pop music!

Splash eats one more fish.

Click! Click!

Layla and the Bots change the music whenever Splash starts squeaking. They get Splash to eat five more fish.

Dr. Sophie returns. The Surfside Rescue Center is closing for the day. It's time to go home.

Thank you for your help today, Layla and the Bots!

But Layla is still worried about Splash.

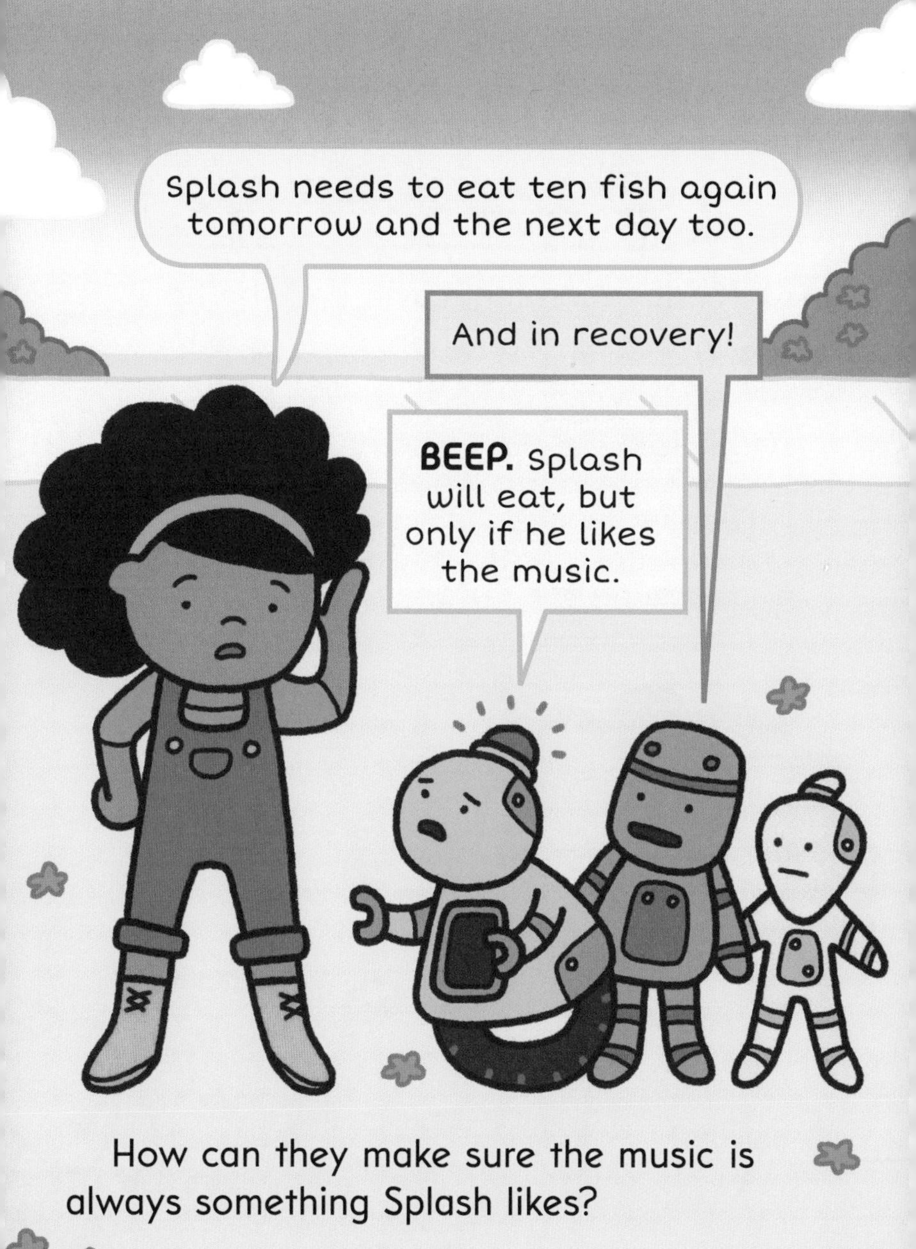
Splash needs to eat ten fish again tomorrow and the next day too.
And in recovery!
BEEP. Splash will eat, but only if he likes the music.

How can they make sure the music is always something Splash likes?

5
THINK TANK

On Friday morning, Layla and the Bots hurry to their workshop.

Splash is picky about the music he wants to hear. What if we build a way for him to choose his own music? Then he will eat plenty of fish, and be strong enough for surgery AND recovery!

Brainstorm time!

They think and sketch.

Then they share their ideas.

Okay, what do you have?

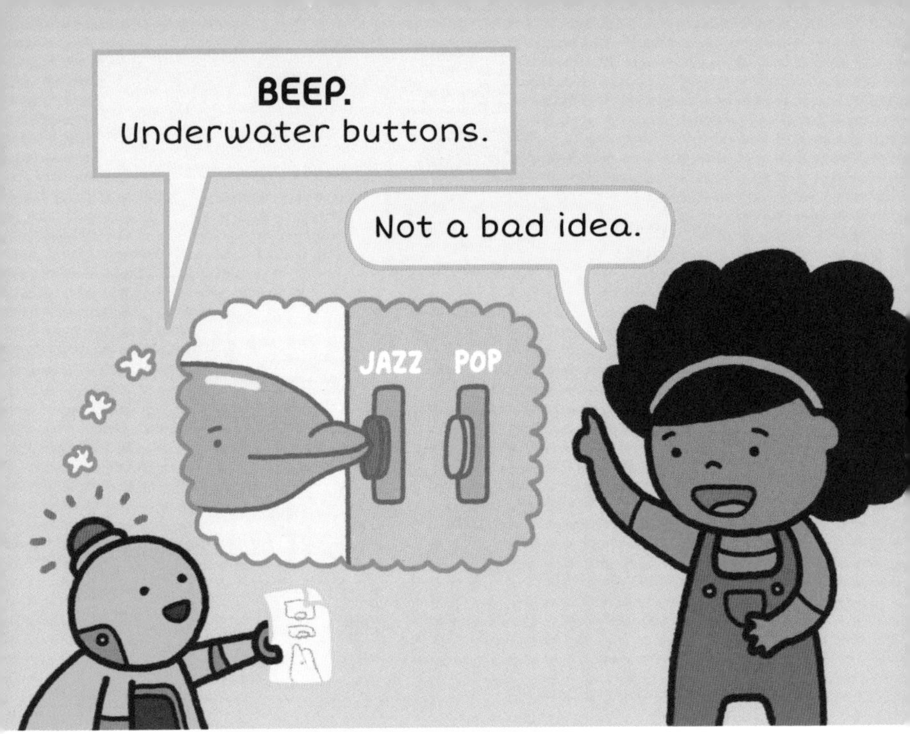
BEEP.
Underwater buttons.
Not a bad idea.
JAZZ
POP

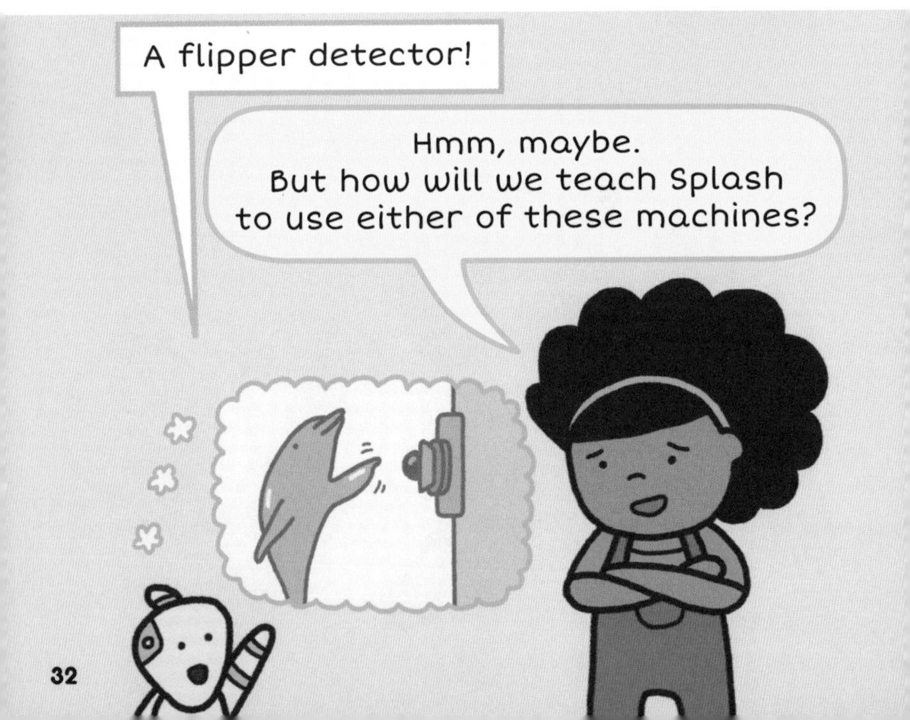
A flipper detector!
Hmm, maybe. But how will we teach Splash to use either of these machines?

We know Splash squeaks when he's upset. What about a squeak detector?

Layla jumps up and gives Boop a big hug.

That's perfect! We code the computer to change the music when Splash squeaks. That way, we don't have to teach Splash how to use our machine. It will just work for him!

Layla sketches out a diagram.

Layla and the Bots study the diagram.

But how will the computer know when a sound is a squeak?

And not just talking?

Or singing?!

Layla frowns. The Bots are right. How can they make the computer detect only Splash's squeaks?

6
MAKING WAVES

Layla and the Bots think while they eat lunch.

We need to find a way for the computer to figure out when Splash is squeaking.

How can we tell the computer what a squeak sounds like?

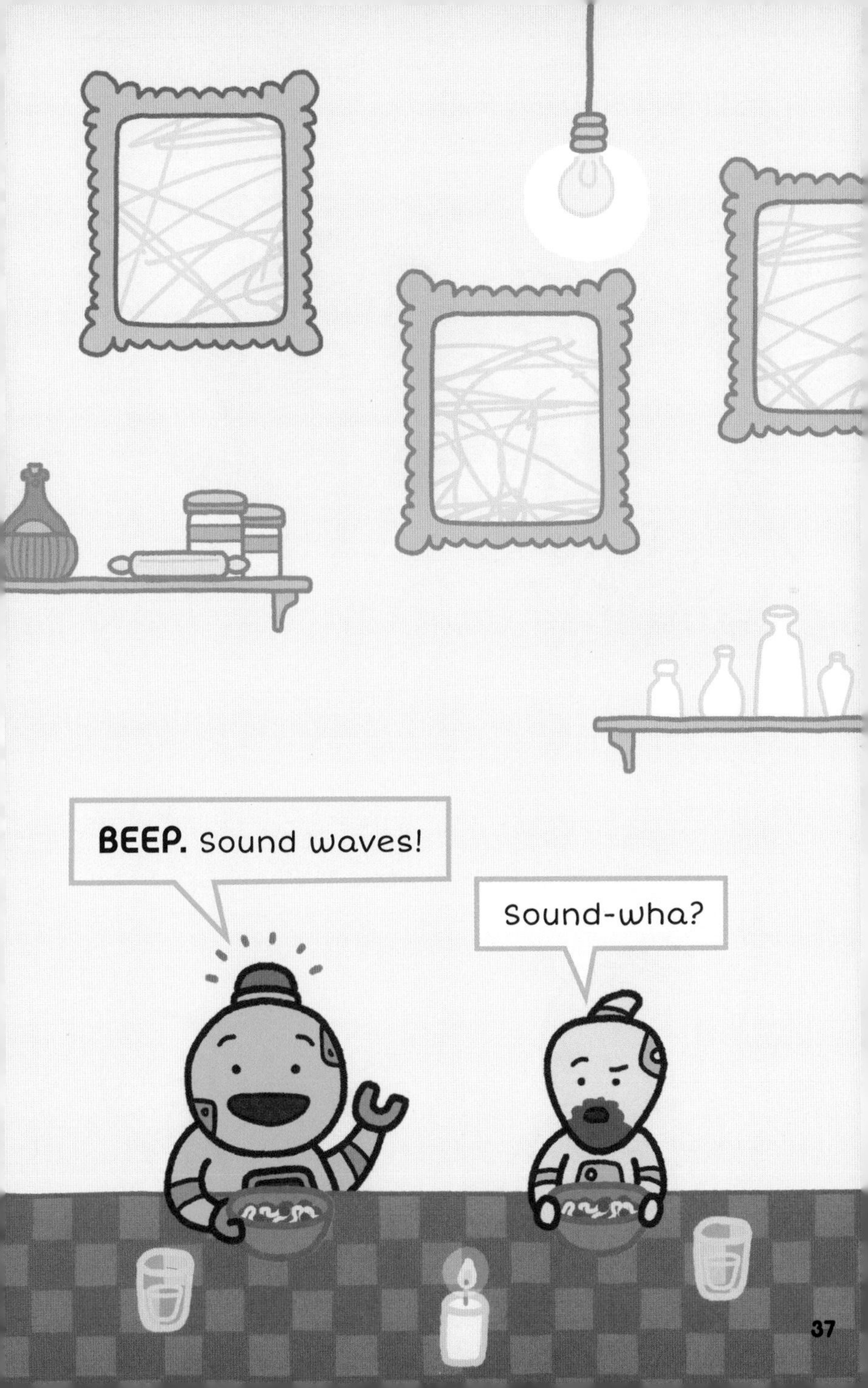
BEEP. Sound waves!
Sound-wha?

BEEP. Sound is made by vibrations in the air.

Beep pulls out a noodle from his lunch.

They travel through the air in a wave! Like this.

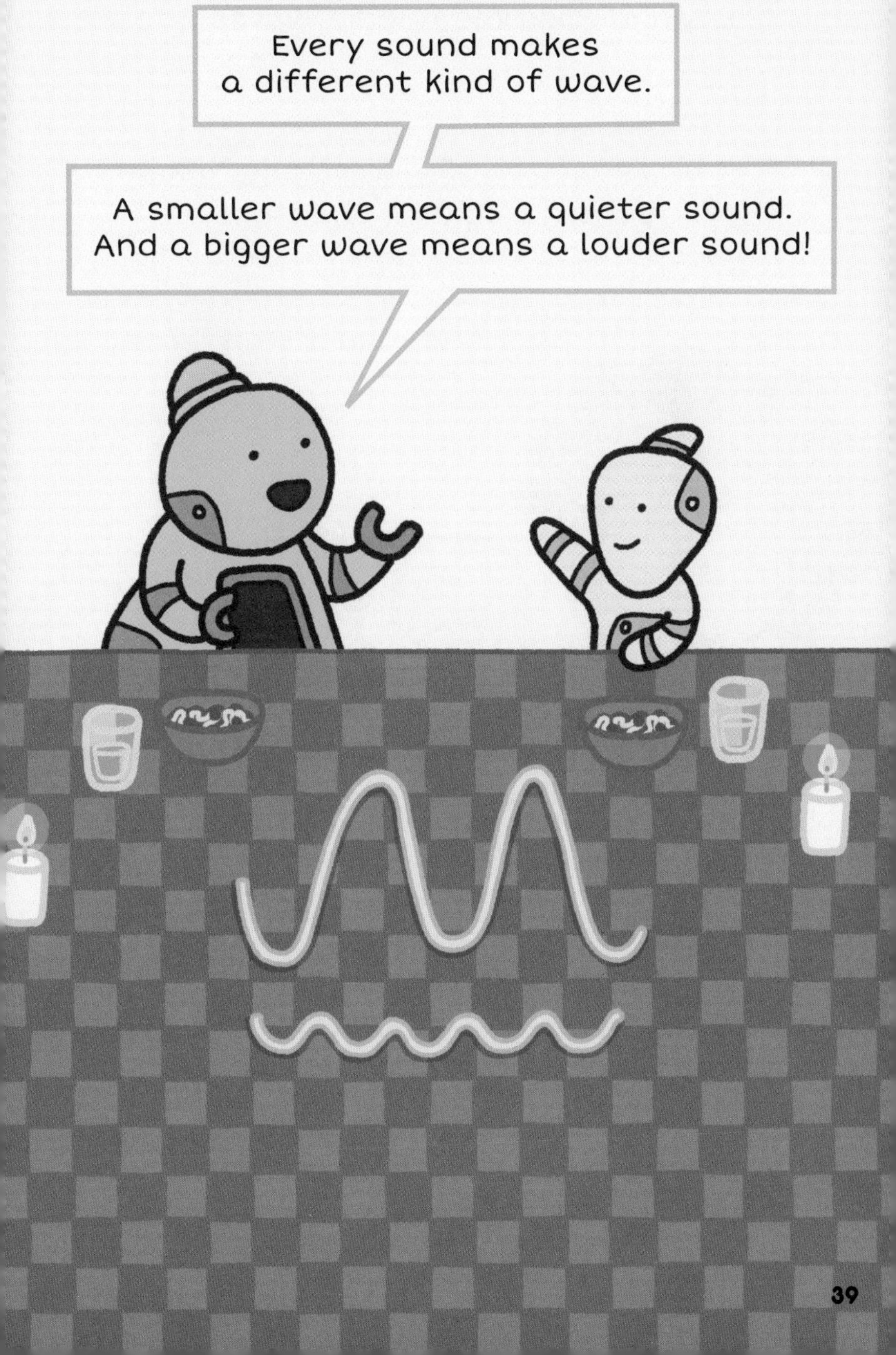
Every sound makes a different kind of wave.
A smaller wave means a quieter sound. And a bigger wave means a louder sound!

Layla studies the noodle waves.

So if we know what the sound wave for Splash's squeak looks like . . .

And how it's different from our voices . . .

We can tell the computer how to detect his squeaks!

Layla stands up.

We've got to get back to the center to record some squeaks!

Back at the Surfside Rescue Center,
Beep records Splash squeaking.

Squeak! Squeak!

Then, he records Layla and the Bots talking and singing.

They compare the sound waves.

BEEP. Splash's squeak sound wave is much <u>bigger</u> than our sound waves.

That means his squeaks are <u>louder</u> than our noises!

Perfect! If a sound is loud enough, we know it's a squeak!

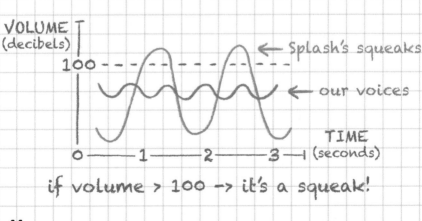

VOLUME (decibels)

100 - - - - - - - - - - - - - - - -   ← Splash's squeaks

← our voices

TIME (seconds)

0 —— 1 —— 2 —— 3 —

if volume > 100 -> it's a squeak!

Layla and the Bots keep feeding Splash until it's time to go home.

That's ten fish! Good work today, Bots. Tomorrow, we build!

7
SOMETHING FISHY

On Saturday morning, Layla and the Bots build in their workshop.

Let's start!

Beep double-checks the diagrams.

Boop gathers the parts.

Bop practices his dance moves while his computers boot up.

First, they set up the squeak detector.
Beep double-checks the sound wave for
Splash's squeak.

Boop builds the waterproof microphone.

Bop writes the code to identify Splash's squeak.

Then, they set up the music player.
Beep puts together some playlists.

Pop, jazz, disco, and . . .
Layla and the Bots!

Boop builds the speakers.

Bop codes the computer to change music when Splash squeaks.

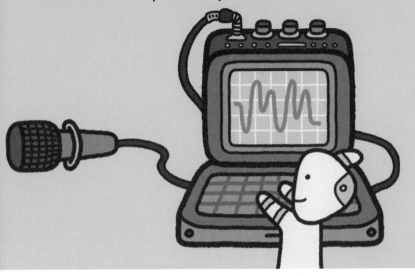

I love it!

Layla and the Bots hurry to Splash's pool. It's almost closing time.

Bop boots up the computer. Music starts playing.

Up and running!

Splash squeaks.

Squeak!

They all hold their breath. . .

And the music changes! They cheer as Splash starts clicking.

Click! Click!

Boop throws him a fish. Splash eats it.

But then the music changes again.

Why did the music change? Splash didn't squeak.

Splash starts squeaking and zooms around the pool, upset. The music changes again and again!

What's going on?

BEEP. The music is only supposed to change when Splash squeaks! NOT when he clicks!

Layla's heart beats fast. Splash's surgery is tomorrow! They need to fix the music machine to make sure he's happy and eats ten fish today. What is wrong with their music machine?

8
FINE-TUNING

Layla and the Bots look over the machine.
Beep checks the squeak detector.

Something's wrong!
What could it be?

BEEP. I know what it is.
I forgot about the clicks!

Beep draws in his notebook.

Splash's clicks are so loud, the click
sound waves look like squeaks.
So the computer changes the music
when it hears both squeaks <u>and</u> clicks!

Our code catches sounds louder
than the dotted line.

Splash's squeaks   Splash's clicks

VOLUME
(decibels)
100 - - - - - - - - - - - - - - - - -

0 ——— 1 ——— 2 ——— 3 —|

TIME
(seconds)

But Splash's clicks and squeaks
are the same volume.

Layla stares at Beep's notebook.

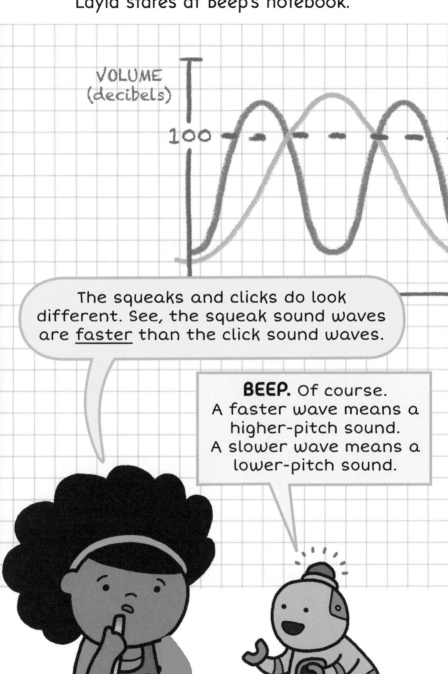

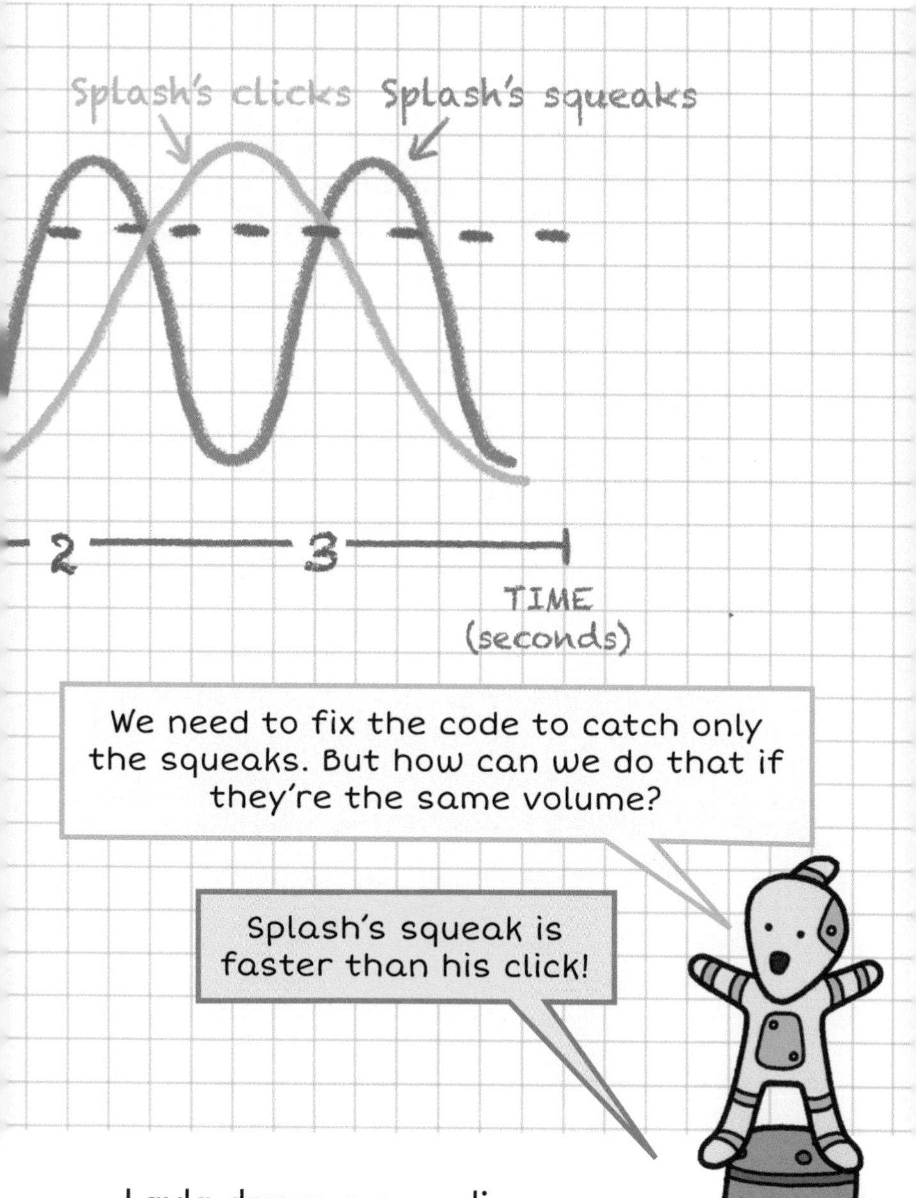
Splash's clicks
Splash's squeaks
2
3
TIME
(seconds)
We need to fix the code to catch only the squeaks. But how can we do that if they're the same volume?
Splash's squeak is faster than his click!

Layla draws a new diagram.

SQUEAK DETECTOR

Update the code to check for sounds that are loud (tall waves) AND fast (quick waves)!

SQUEAK!
CLICK!

if volume > 100
AND speed > 50 -> it's a squeak!

if squeak -> change music!

If we measure how big AND fast the squeak sound wave is, then we can detect only his squeaks!

Bop makes the updates to the code.
Layla restarts the machine, and music
begins playing.

Splash squeaks . . . and the music
changes!

Squeak!
Squeak!

Then he clicks. The music stays the same!

Look, Splash is happy!

And our new code worked!

Whoop-yay!

Splash eats three fish.

Dr. Sophie comes by.

Wow, Splash looks really strong!
Nice work, Layla and the Bots.

Layla beams.

If your machine keeps working and Splash eats six more fish, then he'll be cleared for surgery tomorrow!

Yay-yay!

But as they head home, Layla's tummy flutters like seaweed. Will their invention be enough to help Splash?

9
MAKING A SPLASH!

On Sunday morning, Layla and the Bots rush to the center.

Did our machine work?

Was Splash able to have surgery?

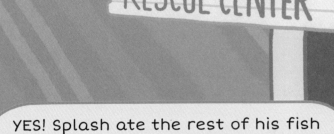

YES! Splash ate the rest of his fish last night, so we were able to do the surgery early this morning. It was a huge success! Come say hello.

Layla and the Bots head to Splash's pool. He is clicking and listening to his Layla and the Bots playlist!

Thank you, Layla and the Bots! Your machine saved the day. I'm sure that Splash will keep eating and get even stronger as he recovers from the surgery. Then we can release him back into the wild!

Click! Click!

Layla and the Bots cheer! They give Splash a high five.

Then, the fundraiser begins!

It's time for our show!

Dr. Sophie opens the gate to the big pool. Splash swims out as Layla and the Bots rush onto the stage.

It was Layla and the Bots' splashiest show ever.

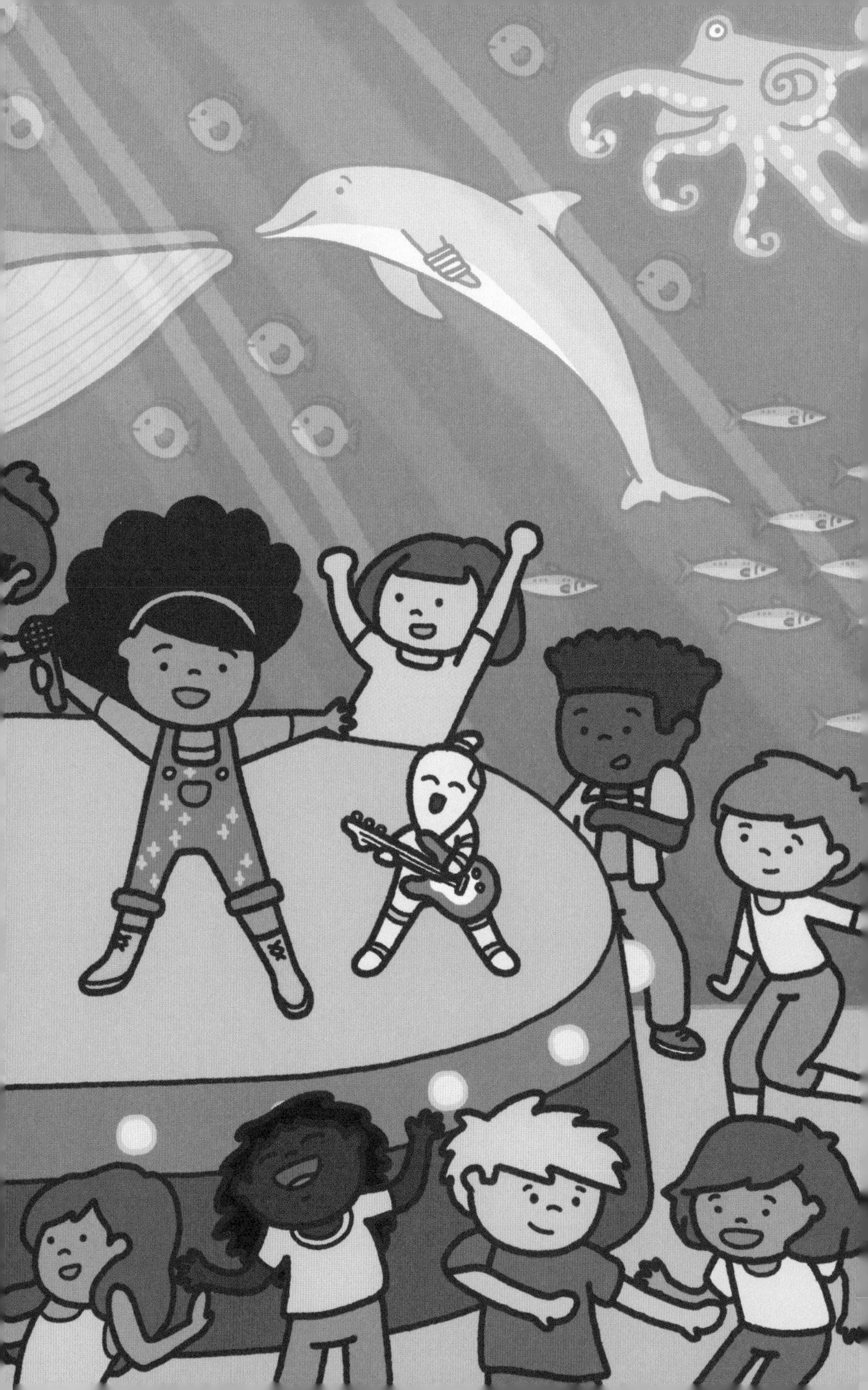

DESIGN AND BUILD YOUR OWN

YOU'LL NEED THE FOLLOWING ITEMS:

- Small/medium cardboard box
  (bigger than a pencil case, but
  smaller than a backpack)
- 3 or more rubber bands
- Scissors
- Decorative craft supplies (optional)

STEP 1. BUILD THE INSTRUMENT

- Open the cardboard box.
  Cut off the lid/flaps on
  the open end. (Make sure the
  other end of the box is taped.)
  This box is now the body of your
  instrument.

- Wrap rubber bands around the box so
  they stretch across the open side.

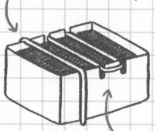

TIP: If your rubber bands are too small, you
can cut slits along the open edge of the
box to hold the rubber bands in place.
You'll need four slits in total for each
rubber band. Leave several inches between
each slit.

MUSICAL INSTRUMENT!

STEP 2. TEST AND FIX

- Try it out! Strum your rubber bands to make music.

- Experiment to make different sounds. What do thicker rubber bands sound like? What happens when a rubber band is stretched farther?

- Cut new slits to make patterns with your rubber bands. How does this change the sound?

- Move your rubber bands around until you're happy with the way your instrument sounds.

STEP 3. ROCK OUT!

- Decorate your awesome instrument and make it your own. You can use markers, stickers, feathers, googly eyes — whatever you like!

- Draw a picture of your final design.

- Put on a show! Show off your new instrument with a performance.

HOW MUCH DO YOU KNOW ABOUT MAKING WAVES?

Look back to page 16. Why isn't Splash eating? What does Splash need to do so that he can be strong for surgery?

How does Splash communicate his feelings? Is this similar to other animals that you know?

What are sound waves? How is the sound wave for a <u>quiet</u> sound different than the wave for a <u>loud</u> sound?

Why can't the music machine tell the difference between Splash's <u>squeaks</u> and <u>clicks</u>? How do Layla and the Bots solve the problem?

The Surfside Rescue Center helped Splash get better after he ate plastic in the ocean. Research two ways that you can help protect the ocean! Write and draw a description of your plan.

ABOUT THE CREATORS

VICKY FANG is a product designer who has designed things like cardboard robots, books that play sound effects, and competitive pinball machines. She's never designed a music player for a dolphin . . . but she has designed music players for humans! Vicky lives in California with her husband and kids. LAYLA AND THE BOTS is her first early chapter book series.

CHRISTINE NISHIYAMA is an artist who draws all sorts of stuff in her sketchbook. She's passionate about helping others discover their own way of drawing. Christine

lives in North Carolina with her husband, dog, and toddler, Butterbean. Christine is also the author and illustrator of the picture book WE ARE FUNGI.

READ MORE LAYLA and the BOTS BOOKS!

BRANCHES
LAYLA and the BOTS
HAPPY PAWS
written by Vicky Fang
illustrated by Christine Nishiyama
SCHOLASTIC
1

BRANCHES
LAYLA and the BOTS
BUILT FOR SPEED
written by Vicky Fang
illustrated by Christine Nishiyama
SCHOLASTIC
2

BRANCHES
LAYLA and the BOTS
CUPCAKE FIX
written by Vicky Fang
illustrated by Christine Nishiyama
SCHOLASTIC
3

BRANCHES
LAYLA and the BOTS
MAKING WAVES
written by Vicky Fang
illustrated by Christine Nishiyama
SCHOLASTIC
4

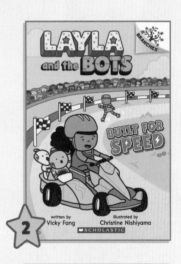

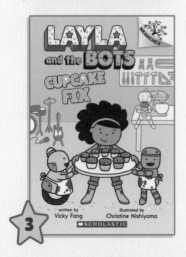